TERRY THE TERRIBLE ELF

Including Terry the Terrible Elf: Lockdown

Joshua Potts

Copyright © 2020 Joshua Potts

All rights reserved

Cover design by: Joshua Potts
Printed in the United Kingdom

CONTENTS

TERRY THE TERRIBLE ELF

O n one cold Christmas morning in the North Pole, an elf was crying in his bedroom. He had refused to join the Successful Christmas Delivery Celebrations. He had pushed all of his presents aside, telling himself that he didn't deserve them.

There was a knock at the door.

The elf used his stocking to dry his eye and said "Go away. I don't want to talk to anyone."

(I'm sure you agree, boys and girls, that this was very rude and neither you nor I would ever speak to someone this way, but we need to remember how upset this elf was.)

"Well someone wants to talk to you, Terry."

"I'll talk to them tomorrow."

"Ho ho ho!" a great voice boomed. "Is that any attitude to have on Christmas day?"

Holy Sprouts! It was! It was Santa Claus!

He shrank to fit into the elf's little room. (What's that? You didn't know that Santa could shrink? Of course he shrinks. How else would he fit down the chimney after so many mince pies?)

Terry was too ashamed to look but Santa laughed.

"Ho ho ho! It sounds to me as though you've had a very eventful Christmas, little elf."

Terry nodded timidly.

"You can say that again, Mr Claus."

"Indeed! Ho ho ho! Why don't you tell me all about it? Start at the beginning."

Terry took his stocking and blew his nose. Tears gone, he turned to face Santa Claus.

Well, sir. You see-"

* * *

I'm terribly sorry, boys and girls, but I'm afraid that I'm required to interrupt Terry here. You see, just as toys require batteries, stories require things before they will work properly too. For our purposes, I think we ought to know a little bit more about what sort of elf Terry was. If you know what had come before, you might find Terry's actions, while still wrong, understandable. So, while Terry tells his story from the beginning, we are going to go *before* the beginning. Don't worry. We'll meet up with him soon.

Terry was a terrible elf. A *truly* terrible elf. Oh, in some ways he was just like the others. His favourite food ever was mince pies. He wore the usual green and red uniform and his absolute favourite time of year was Christmas. Terry's problem, however, was that he was... well, terrible. Final copies of the nice list were given out in November, but no matter how many times Terry read it, the toys that he built always went wrong. Sure, he had the best of intentions. He wanted nothing more than to give every kiddie everything that their heart desired. He built with love, but perhaps a little too much love. A carelessness of love made him clumsy. The chocolates that Terry put in the advent calendars were always sickeningly sweet. Any eggnog he brewed resulted in a potency decreed to be *festively fatal.*

The same goes for the sprouts...

Well, boys and girls, you can imagine how difficult this was for Terry, being so bad at Christmas when he loved it with all his heart. He was simply over-eager. It's all well and good saying, "It's the thought that counts", but what are you supposed to do when your stockings are on fire and the kitchen walls are lined with bacon? He meant his best but he got too excited. If you have ever heard Christmas carols playing in a supermarket before October, you can bet that Terry has been there.

One year, the elves decided that they couldn't sugar-coat the situation any longer. (And elves *love* to sugar-coat things, so that's how bad things were!) They tried to ask Santa's advice but it was too close to Christmas and he was busy checking his lists. "I swear the only reason he checks the list more than once is so he doesn't have to help with the heavy lifting," moaned Cormac MacSugarcane.

The elves decided to bring the problem to Mrs Claus. Everyone knew that she was the fairest and most patient person in the North Pole.

"Well," said Mrs Claus, "We all love Terry. I say we speak to him, and explain this directly but calmly." So that's exactly what they did.

"Terry, we all love you, and we need to speak to you. We're going to go around the circle and tell you how your Christmas excitement is causing us problems."

"Problems? But it's Christmas, and I -"

"Fer the love of parsnips, lad!" said MacSugarcane, as tactfully as he could manage. "This has got to stop.

Yer gonna kill one of us if you carry on how you are."

"I'm afraid," said Mrs Claus, "it would be better for everyone, Terry, for you to stop working in the toy factory."

"But Mother Christmas - Mrs Nick - Miss Claus - Ma'am. Christmas is my life. I can't not be a Christmas elf. I just can't!"

The elves smiled sadly. Poor Terry. *It wasn't his fault, but what could they do?*

"Please give me another chance. I just need time to learn."

"With the greatest of respect, little elf, you have been with us for many Christmases. We had really expected you to grow out of your training ears years ago."

"Terry," said Nimbles, Terry's very best friend in the whole world, "I'm afraid the rest of us just can't afford to keep fixing your mistakes."

"But, I-" Terry had no answer to this. *Maybe he shouldn't be a Christmas elf.*

"I'll pack my things."

"No no no, we didn't mean that," said Mrs Claus, with perhaps more sympathy than sense. "I think you might say that we haven't quite discovered the best ribbon for your particular - ahem- gift."

So, the search for Terry's true calling began. He started out by stocking advent calendars but Terry couldn't resist putting all of the chocolates in the number 1 door. Then, Terry had a job feeding the reindeer but he ended up riding them all over the North Pole that they were going to be too tired to ride on Christmas Eve. Finally, with nowhere else to put him, Terry was asked to sweep snow from in front of the workshop, "for the time being". He was true to his word for as long as he could manage but he found it too hard to hold back once the Christmas period had arrived. (Which, for Terry, was in the middle of August.)

So, Terry hatched a plan. A merry plan. A jolly plan!

Oh, they'll see! he thought. *I'll take one family and give them the greatest Christmas anyone ever saw. Then all the elves will take back what they said, and Terry the Terrific Elf will be asked to organise Christmas forever!*

I think boys and girls, that this is enough to give you a good idea of who Terry is, for now. Let's catch up to him as I said, and I will let Terry take the story from here...

"And so, Santa, what I did was this:

* * *

"At night, just before all the other elves had gone to bed, I made a snow-elf and put it in my bed so that the others would think that I was still there. I knew that my sheets would be wet and cold afterwards, but Christmas is worth it. I only felt bad thinking that the other elves might think that I was ignoring them, which of course I wasn't. They would probably think that I was just upset, I told myself.

"When I left, I grabbed a secret stash of presents that I had built myself."

Santa raised his eyebrows questioningly but he didn't look mad.

"I had set up a little private workshop in an empty igloo just on the other side of the pole, Sir. I built the exact presents that were on the list.

"*The Kringles,* I told myself, *are going to have the biggest, most fantastic Christmas that anyone had.*"

"The Kringles?" asked Santa with a knowing look in his eyes. "I don't appear to have them here on my lists, naughty or nice." The elves nodded, confused.

"Yes, well. I wanted to do this alone, you see. So, I... took them off the list. I knew that it wouldn't cause any harm because it wasn't as though they wouldn't be getting any presents. They just wouldn't be... from you, Santa. I alone would handle the Kringles' Christmas. Look here. This is my nice list. It has only five members. Christopher and Nicola Kringle, the boy, the girl and the little baby.

"I knew there would be panic if I took one of the reindeer, so I took the elf snow-car. I must admit, I set off in an excited rush. I went over a snow dune and some of the presents fell out and were scuffled. I put them back in the trailer and drove more carefully. I even scattered them with magic dust, to make them better."

"Magic dust! You did go through my stores!" scolded Rickity Elf. "You know full well that one magic dust is not the same as another."

"Well I know that now! The presents were glowing by the time that I reached the Kringles' house. I just assumed that the presents were as excited as I was. Oh, I'm such a silly elf!

"As I've already said, I was determined that this should be the greatest Christmas anyone in the world ever had. Ever! You should have seen how carefully I hung the stockings at the feet of their beds. I bit off the end of the carrot the boys had left out for Rudolph and I even wrote them a letter from you, Santa, so that they would think that you had been. I laid out their presents and prepared a lovely Christmas CD to wake them up in the morning. And with my work complete, I left in such high spirits."

"Ah, wait one moment there." said Rickity. "That was not all you did, was it? The elves tell me that the house was covered head to toe in magic dust!"

"Yes, well I may have scattered some on the tree just to make it... pop. "

"Pop? You made the tree pop alright! And the turkey. And Mr Kringle's tie. And the front door! No wonder they weren't in their right minds! Everyone within a five-mile radius of that house was intoxicated with... with Christmas spirit!"

"And what's wrong with a little Christmas Spirit?" Terry cried in earnest.

The tips of Rickity Elf's ears turned red and his shoes uncurled.

"All I can say, Terry, is that it's a very good thing that we were out looking for you."

"You were looking for me?"

"Ho ho ho!" chuckled Santa. "Did you not think that we might have been worried about you when you went missing?"

"We're your family, Terry," said Rickity. "We all came up with some Christmas cake for you. We wanted to make sure you were okay. But once we realised what had happened, we had to send in the SWAT elves to resolve the situation!"

Terry felt so guilty. They had really known how upset he was and wanted to make it better. And the SWAT elves. Boy, it must have been a real disaster!

Oh, but what a disaster it was! They ran around on Christmas day in a panic, careful not to knock into any of the humans. The Kringles and their guests had no idea because the elves were invisible. As we all know, an elf must never be seen by children without express permission of the parent, headmaster or mall supervisor.

They replaced the old batteries that Terry had put into the remote-controlled cars. They removed the stocking fillers that Terry had lovingly included in the roast turkey.

Alas! All their hard and well-planned work could not save Christmas for the Kringles. You see, boys and girls, some human grown-ups are so stubborn and hard hearted that they will be unhappy even when things are perfect. Even on Christmas day! Grown-ups are like that. And this is exactly what was happening.

It began pleasantly enough; Mr Kringle (the father of the household) stood up to tell a joke that he had written. It was about two reindeer and a set of golf clubs and it may have been very funny. However, Mr Kringle was so nervous, that he "umm"ed and "ah-h"ed and said "Oh no, I forgot to tell you about the-" Poor Mr Kringle! It did not come across well.

Some laughed politely, but Benjamin (a relation of Mrs Kringle, who was invited because "He has no one else!") burped most unfestively and told Mr Kringle exactly what he thought of his joke.

Oh! Everyone erupted into disagreement. Some rushed to Mr Kringle's defence. Some joined Benjamin in insulting the poor man. Terry thought to himself that it hadn't been such a bad little joke.

Sprouts were thrown, mash was slapped and carrots were snapped in the sort of rage that only a family on Christmas day can have for each other.

"I've got to do something!" said Terry. "I know! Just let me fix this."

"No!" cried the other elves in unison, scooping mint sauce out of some stockings. "Just let the professionals deal with this. Wait with the sleigh."

But Terry loved Christmas too much to give up on it now! He pulled out his last bag of magic dust and blew it all around the dinner table. As if from nowhere, a colourful paper tube appeared in front of each person's plate. You must remember, boys and girls, that this was a long time ago. I'm sure that you know exactly what a Christmas cracker is but the Kringles had no idea. They stopped arguing to have a look. When they sat down and the magic dust took its effect, they all suddenly knew just what to do. They began passing the crackers round and seeing what was inside of them after they went "bang".

Benjamin pulled his cracker by himself - for no one loved him enough to pull it for him - and tore his paper hat over his swollen head. He became very angry at this and the elves worried that another fight was going to break out.

Terry clicked his fingers and a scrap of paper fell from Benjamin's cracker. The elves gasped.

"What have you done?" Padre Elf demanded.

Benjamin picked up the paper.

"Oh, it's a joke!" he said. "I'll read it out. It'll definitely be funnier than yours, Mr Kringle."

And read it out, he did. I shan't print the joke here. It was truly terrible in a way that you are better off not knowing.

One of the elves began to cry. Another collapsed. He was carried up the chimney by two members of the National Elf Service.

A SWAT elf turned to Terry very angrily and said,

"Haven't you caused enough trouble for us, Terence? Take the snow car. And. Go. Home." Ashamed, Terry left, looking no one in the eye. He was such a bad elf! He had really done it. Terry, the terrible elf, had ruined Christmas!

"Ho ho ho! So, you really planned to save Christmas by telling a little joke, did you, little elfling?"

Terry's lip wobbled.

"Yes, but only because this family was in chaos. I know I messed everything up but they were at each other's throats. I thought a joke would cheer them up... What happened? Have they all killed one another?"

Santa Claus lifted his head back and laughed. It was a deep and joyful laugh.

"Ho ho ho! Killed, I think not, my lad. Not in the slightest. The furthest thing from it."

Terry sat up with hope.

"Do you mean that they found my joke funny?"

Santa turned to the elves and said "Not exactly, no. Nimbles, perhaps you would explain."

"Well, Terry,' said Nimbles. "When they read your

joke, they all... groaned."

"Groaned?"

"Yes, they were rather taken aback by just how bad it was."

Terry sank.

"But that's just the thing!" he added quickly. "They groaned and said it was bad. Truly awful. The worst joke anyone had ever been cruel enough to conceive of."

Terry began to cry again at this and Santa prompted, "That's quite enough. Get on with the main bit, Nimbles."

"Oh yes, they said... all that. And they agreed. For once in the whole year, they agreed on something. They seem to be getting on marvellously now."

"Because of my bad joke?"

"Ho ho ho, because of your bad joke!"

"So, we've been talking-"

Santa put a big warm hand on his shoulder.

"Terence Elfus Terribilis. I would like you to be our official Christmas cracker joke teller! On two conditions... First, you leave all the toy construction and delivery to us. Secondly, and more importantly...

Every joke you tell must be as terrible as the one you told this morning."

And they certainly were just as terrible. Worse, in fact. Year in, year out!

In fact, Santa was so impressed at what an improvement Terry had made, that he was asked to handle the Kringle Christmas from then on. And year after year, The Kringles groan and say, "What a load of rubbish! I swear they get worse every year." Terry doesn't get upset though, because at this point, Benjamin throws his arm around Mr Kringle and says, "They certainly do, Chris. I tell you what, why don't we open this Brandy of Nicola's and you can tell us some of your own terrific jokes."

Terry runs his own little workshop now. It's a small operation but they take on a few more families every few Christmases. Santa can always tell if a family needs a particular *non-traditional* brand of Christmas and sends them Terry's way. He may drop the presents on his journey. He may leave the house a mess as he rushes about in excitement. But Terry knows that Christmas is really about cosying up together in the ugliest jumpers, telling the stupidest jokes and agreeing what a terrible year it has been, and being all the closer a family for it.

Terry is a terribly wonderful elf.

TERRY THE TERRIBLE ELF: LOCKDOWN

From the pen of Mr. S. Claus,

I'm writing to you, boys and girls, in response to some troubling news that I have received. I have been told about how all the little boys and little girls and mummies and daddies and big brothers and little brothers and big sisters and little sisters and grandmas and granddads and cats and dogs and goldfish all have to stay at home. I bet it must be very boring but I'll tell you what - I've also been told how good everyone has been, doing their school-work at home, helping Mummy and Daddy with the house, putting up artwork in your windows to thank all the doctors and nurses and everybody else who had been helping poorly people. You should all be very proud of yourselves.

When I was told about this from my executive news elf, I was reminded of something that once happened to an elf called Terry. Oh, do you already know Terry? Well, if you don't, Terry is one of our greatest Christmas elves - and if you haven't heard of him, I bet you've pulled one of those excellent Christmas crackers that he invented! You see, Terry once went through a time - well - very similar to the one that you are experiencing right now. And he found it tough, but he focused on those he loved and worked really hard just like you have and - well, perhaps I should just tell the story.

This is what happened when, all over the North Pole, everyone was catching sniffling sickness. When elves have sniffling sickness, it is impossible for them to make any toys. Their noses run without ever stopping. The North Pole, as you know, is very cold and if an elf is caught outside, his runny nose would turn to ice!

When sniffling sickness first came to the North Pole, I had to put up posters, which told everyone how to stay safe. They had to wash their hands for as long as it took them to sing their favourite Christmas carol. We placed soap at the entrance to every workshop. This alone caused a problem. You see, Elven soap is flavoured like bubble-gum and it wasn't long before elves were eating them. It was chaos!

The elves were asked very gently and yet very firmly that they don't go to any parties. Well, they certainly tried, but an elf that doesn't go to parties is like a duck that doesn't go in the water. Elves live their lives like one long Christmas party and there were some very frowny faces at this sad news.

And this is the story of when the workshop had to close for a little while and all the elves had to go back to live with their families. They had to pack their suitcases full of gadgets and gizmos so that they could continue to build toys at home. It had been a long time since Terry had visited his family because he was so busy with Christmas preparations. In truth, Terry was a bit nervous about going home. Things were so different there than they were at the North Pole. You see, not all elves become Christmas elves. Terry was actually one of the few who left Elfwood to join Santa's workshop- but that's a tale for another time.

When Terry was nearly home, he was feeling sad. He didn't know how long it would be until he got to make Christmas presents again. He decided that he would cheer himself up by visiting the house of his favourite human family. These were the Kringles.

Terry's fans will remember that his unusual yet jolly treatment of the Kringle family Christmas is what led to his position as a specialist Christmas day planner. You see, the family were having a terrible row- which is not what we want on Christmas day, is it?- and in that moment, Terry thought that a joke would lighten the mood. The problem was that Terry's joke was not very funny (by human standards). The Kringle family groaned at the joke and complained about it and yet somehow this shared complaint brought them closer together. Terry now led a team who oversaw the Kringle family Christmas every year. At least he had until the workshop had been closed down.

When Terry reached the Kringles' house, he used his elf magic to enter very, very quietly. It was night time and they were sure to all be in bed.

"Oh Terry," he told himself. "Maybe this isn't such a good idea. You'd better come back in the morning." However, as Terry was leaving, he heard a noise. He looked into one of the children's bedrooms and saw that all three of them were sat on the bed looking very sad indeed.

The Kringles have three children. The eldest is a pretty girl called Erin, who has a lovely singing voice. She was eleven years old at the time. Her younger brother is called Charlie and he was nine years old in this story. Charlie loves everything to do with science and has read every book he owns at least twice. The youngest of the Kringle children is little Lou, who was only five years old when she sat sadly with her brother and sister on the bed. Lou loved her brother and sister very much and liked to do whatever they were doing. At the moment, that thing was being sad, so being sad was what she was doing.

 Another elf might have thought twice and decided to give the children some privacy, but not Terry! Terry's job was to cheer people up when they were sad and that was what he was best at. In fact, Terry was bending the rules about being seen by humans, but I won't tell if you won't. He had visited the Kringle children many times and he cared about them a great deal. He had never seen them like this before. He went into the bedroom wearing his kindest smile and asked the children what was wrong.

 Lou told Terry that they were very sad that they were not allowed to go see their grandparents any more. They had to stay inside the house except for going for one hour's exercise outside. Erin wiped some tears off of Charlie's cheek.

 "And what's worst of all," sobbed Charlie, "is that it's my birthday next week. And I want my grandma and granddad to be there. But they can't come to our house."

Oh no, thought Terry. *How sad!*

He reminded Charlie that birthdays were still very exciting. "Think about all the presents that you'll get to open in the morning."

"Well... I don't think I'm going to get any presents," he replied. "All of the shops are shut. I won't get any proper presents until the elves bring them on Christmas eve."

Now, Terry felt very sad! He didn't know when the workshop was going to reopen so he didn't know when he and the other elves would be able to bring presents to the children. *Hmmm...* he thought. *What cheered them up last time?*

"I know!" Terry turned his suitcase on its side and pulled out four Christmas crackers. "Let's pull one each. We can wear the funny hats and there might be a little joke inside. Who knows, it might even be a funny one!"

Terry giggled. The children smiled at him politely.

Lou pulled a cracker with Terry. She got the bigger bit.

"You win this one, Lou!" he said. "Let's pop that hat on your head."

Lou sighed sadly and put the hat on. Terry didn't understand it. The cracker was a Christmas thing. Christmas is a jolly time. This should have worked!

He wondered if Christmas magic only worked once a year.

Shortly after, Terry left the Kringles and continued his journey to Elfwood. All the long walk home, he couldn't stop thinking about those poor children. No presents for Charlie's birthday. Maybe no presents for anyone on Christmas day. And above that, they really wanted to see their grandparents and they weren't allowed.

It's just not right, Terry thought.

Terry loved his own family very much; but he was nervous because things were so different there. Where Terry was used to a warm fire in the workshop during a whirling blizzard, most elves in the forest live in hollowed-out trees. Terry didn't find these cosy at all. In fact, they gave him splinters on his bottom whenever he sat down.

Terry had been quite unusual for wanting to be a Christmas elf. Most of his brothers (he had about a hundred or so but he always lost count) preferred to go off adventuring with the dwarves in the mountains. What's the fun in all that? Terry thought. There's never any chocolate on those adventures either. No, I'm perfectly happy being a Christmas elf. He had shined his Specialist Elf badge for the visit. He had packed his suitcase with the crackers so that he could show them successful he was.

This was his first mistake. Oh sure, it was a nice thought. And Terry's daddy loved him so much that he would have been proud of Terry, whether he understood what he was being shown or not. But the journey to Elfwood was hard and bumpy and it set off one of Terry's Christmas crackers with a Bang! This triggered another bang, which in turn, set off several more. Soon Terry's entire suitcase exploded in a blaze of light and sent Terry rolling down the mountain in a ball of snow. Faster and faster he rolled, seeing nothing, growing dizzier all the while. Terry felt himself stop suddenly and heard a crash. He lay at the base of the tallest tree you ever saw. Laying on the ground, Terry could -see it reaching up into the sky and past the clouds.

He was home.

Terry's father had prepared a wonderful meal for the family. It reminded Terry of being a young elfling again. They ate outside the tree, on the floor, like a huge picnic. There was not room to eat inside because elves have hundreds and hundreds of children. Out of Terry's four hundred siblings, he was the very middle child.

They held a huge feast in the forest to celebrate Terry's return. A group of elves played their music and everyone danced around the fire. The pixies, which are like elves but they can fly and are very

very beautiful, performed beautiful dances in the sky.

There was one pixie there who was not in Terry's family. She was called Tilly, and Terry had always considered her the most beautiful pixie that he had ever seen in his life. A lot of elves thought so actually, but she didn't pay them any mind. Tilly had pretty blue wings that curved at the corners when she laughed. Should I let you in on a little secret, boys and girls? Will you promise not to laugh? When Terry had lived in Elfwood, he had once given Tilly a kiss on the cheek under the fairy lights. That had been the day before Terry became a Christmas elf.

Terry was deciding what he could say to Tilly without his tongue turning into knots when she picked him up and the two of them danced in the sky. They swung round and round and laughed and Terry tried to remember all his old dance moves from when he was a young elfling. He even threw in a few of his North Pole dances and everyone laughed.

"You're so silly, Terry," Tilly said to him when they had come back down to the ground.

"Why am I silly?"

"The way you did that funny jig. Did you learn that at the North Pole?"

"Yes," Terry said. "It's a Christmas dance. All the

elves do it. All the Christmas elves, I mean."

"You and Christmas, Terry! I'll never understand."

That comment gave Terry a plan.

That night, after all the elves and pixies and everyone else had gone to sleep, he and Tilly snuck out to give everyone a nice surprise.

"I still don't understand, Terry," she said.

"You will," he said. "Watch this." He opened his suitcase and pulled out his collection of tree decorations. "We're going to wrap these around that big tree there."

"Why?"

"Trust me. It'll make the tree seem magical."

"But it is magical, Terry. That's where the pixies live."

"Just try it. I promise."

Tilly took a stream of Christmas lights and wrapped them around the tree. She used her wings to fly up and circled the tree, getting higher and higher.

"Wheee!" she called. "This is fun!"

"I told you so!" he said. "But you need to be quiet."

"Why?"

"So that nobody knows that it was us."

"Wheee!" she whispered.

And so, Terry the Terrible Elf and his trusted pixie friend went about setting up the first Christmas that Elfwood had ever seen. They hung stockings at the foot of everyone's bed ("What good is just one sock?" Tilly asked.) and filled them with sweets that Terry had brought in his suitcase.

It was the middle of summer time and there was no snow to be found anywhere. That didn't stop Terry, however. He pulled leaves from the trees and scattered them so that their footsteps made a nice crunching sound. Tilly laughed as he lay down and a- well, I suppose you would call it a leaf angel.

"You're so excited about this, aren't you, Terry?"

"Of course, I am. This is Christmas. This is what I do!"

"Does everyone get as excited as you?"

"Most of them do. Not everyone. People do at the North Pole. And children. Children love Christmas."

"Children?"

"Oh! You don't even know about children, do you? Oh Tilly! Children are the best. You see, children don't stay little forever like elves and pixies. So, when they're small, it's really special. Children are all really imaginative and they love Christmas. Come on, I'll show you my favourites!"

Terry took Tilly to the Kringle house. Fortunately, it didn't take them nearly as long as it had taken Terry the first time because they were able to fly there. On the way, Terry explained all about how the children were sad about having to stay home and that Charlie was worried about not seeing his grandparents on his birthday.

"What's a birthday?"

"Oh Tilly. I keep forgetting about how different things are in Elfwood. Birthdays are amazing. Not as good as Christmas, but they're like mini Christmases that are just for one person. So, every year- a year is when the Earth has spun all the way around once- everyone gets together to celebrate the day that Charlie was born."

"Why? Is Charlie a king or something?"

"No, he's nobody special. I mean, he is. He's amazing. What I mean is that everyone gets a birthday. I mean kings have two, so I suppose that is special in a way."

"And he only has two sisters?"

"That's right."

"Only two? They must be so special to him."

"Oh, they are. They're such good kids. And that's what Christmas is all about. Loving your family. Just see, you're going to love them."

And Tilly did love them! How could she not? The Kringles had raised three very polite and thoughtful children. They read lots of books and this had made them very intelligent. They were, however, still very sad.

"Please tell me why you're so upset," asked Tilly.

The children liked Tilly. They liked how she could fly. They asked why Terry couldn't fly and he explained that he had had to give up his wings to become a Christmas elf. This, they understood. Only adults question people's decisions. Children accept.

Lou explained that her older brother was upset because it was his birthday soon. They were all worried about their grandparents and, on top of that, Charlie was worried that he wouldn't get any birthday presents.

"Well, it's funny you should mention that," Tilly said. She reached into her pocket pouch and pulled out a brown paper package. "Terry mentioned that you were worried about your presents and I wanted to make sure that you would get one, at least."

Charlie hadn't been expecting this. "Thank you," he said, for he was a very polite young man and always remembered his pleases and thank-yous. "You didn't have to bring me a present." He wiped his tears, embarrassed. "I wasn't that upset. I'm a big boy, you know."

"I know you're a big boy. You're much bigger than me!" Tilly was three inches tall when she stood up straight. "But hang on a minute, young man. That's a birthday present. You're going to have to wait. But don't worry, that's not all I was thinking. Now that you're feeling a bit better, why don't we all stand up and sing a song?"

Charlie and his two sisters stood around the shaggy blue rug in the centre of their bedroom. Tilly held out her hands to show them that they needed to form a circle. They had to step a little closer so that they weren't lifting her and Terry above the ground. They spent the morning learning all the songs that elves like to sing at parties. Erin in particular was a wonderful singer but all three children had lots of fun. In return, the children taught the elf and pixie the songs they liked to sing. Lou taught everyone songs from her favourite cartoons. Charlie taught them a rude one that he'd learnt from a boy at school. Terry didn't think it was appropriate but Tilly giggled.

After a wonderful few hours of singing and games, the group sat on the rug tired out but jolly.

"Thank you," Erin said. "You've really cheered us up. And I'm sorry Terry. I know that you were trying to cheer us up, before. I guess we just felt a bit silly doing Christmas things."

"I completely understand. You're a lovely singer, by the way."

"But hang on. I'm confused," said Tilly.

"Why, Tilly?"

"Terry said that on Christmas day, everyone is kind

to each other. That they give presents, play games and sing songs together."

"That's right."

"But isn't that exactly what we've been doing. How is this not Christmas stuff?"

"Well they weren't Christmas songs," said Terry. "They were jolly songs, but Christmas songs are... Well..."

"Christmas songs have Santa in them," said Lou.

"And reindeer" added Charlie.

"Yes, well..." said Terry. "I guess it's complicated."

"I guess it is," concluded Tilly. "But I think we got the important stuff. I think what we had this morning was a... hmm... a "Thismas". You know? Not a special day, but just celebrating today."

Lou giggled. "You're so silly."

"No Lou, I think it's a good idea. Merry Thismas, Tilly." Erin tried to say it seriously but she started giggling too.

They all wished one another a Merry Thismas and they all giggled. Charlie thanked Tilly for his gift one more time and the elves went home to Elfwood.

During the journey home, Terry wondered how the elves would be reacting to their Christmas decorations. The elves were thinking the same.

"What on Earth am I supposed to do with this?" they asked.

"Umm... Terry, why is there a sock at the end of my bed?"

"That's a stocking, Dad."

"Is there only meant to be one? I was wondering if perhaps you had forgotten the other one."

Terry laughed. "No, that's how it's meant to be. There are sweets inside."

"Oh, yes. I see," he said, but he still looked confused. "Why is nobody wearing their jumpers?"

"Well," said one of Terry's brothers. "Mine itches."

"Mine too," someone called.

"And mine!"

"Mine's got an ugly picture of a penguin on the front! I think you need to try again, Terry."

"No, that's how they're meant to be."

"Terry! None of this makes any sense!"

"No. It does. Everyone, just listen. We wear those things because... Well, you know how important it is to love our family, right?"

There were murmurs of agreement.

"Well, that's what Christmas is for."

"But can't I love my family with both my socks on?"

"This jumper is scratching my belly," a pixie shouted.

"Well, then put on a shirt. I..."

Oh dear. Terry's heart was in the right place but he wasn't equipped to explain what Christmas was.

Imagine a fish trying to explain what water is to someone who has been dry their entire life. Well, that's what it was like for Terry. He lived in the North Pole with Father Christmas and all of the other Christmas elves. Everyone loved Christmas and he wasn't used to people not understanding it. Thank goodness that Terry wasn't left to this job alone.

Terry turned around and saw Tilly, hands held behind her back, singing. She was wonderful.

The crowd of elves stopped arguing. One of the old elves joined in with the song. He sang in a low bass rumble. Then others joined. Soon, everyone was singing along holding hands. This was a song that they had heard from their grandparents and had been passed down for generations. Terry joined in as well as he could but felt bad that he had forgotten some of the words. But nobody judged him for it. They were holding hands, singing as one. All of a sudden, they were not singing beside each other, but rather singing together. They stopped being individual elves standing around and they became one group.

The song came to an end with a wonderful harmony.

"Well," one of them said. "Isn't it wonderful to hear that one again?" There were strong notes of agreement from within the crowd. The elf who had spoken started singing another old song. Things were quickening up now into a party. Everyone joined in and swayed.

When this song was over, Terry thought that this was his moment to join in. Deciding against a traditional carol, he started singing the first few lines of Charlie's rude song. It was not well received.

"Excuse me for a moment." He walked away, embarrassed.

"I just want to say something," said Tilly. "I have been trying to understand this Christmas thing, just like the rest of you. And honestly, I'm stumped. I agree with the rest of you. It's ridiculous. But this morning, Terry and I helped some very lovely young humans. We swapped some presents and sang some songs like the silly one you just heard. For me, we got all of that lovely gooey stuff that Terry keeps banging on about but without all the silly jumpers and sprouts. It's just about... well, it's about this." She gestured her hands out to the elves, many of whom were holding on to each other a little tighter now. "I call it Thismas."

There was a pause as people considered what she'd said.

"Silly name that, Tilly," someone shouted.

"Shut up, Alf. She's right."

Tilly turned to smile at Terry but he had gone.

"Everyone, take your seat please!"

Terry had emerged from the tree. At least they assumed it was him. Two oven mitts were lifting the biggest tray of meat they'd ever seen in their life. They could see two little elven legs wiggling underneath it.

"Oh Terry!"

"Please, clear some space."

Quickly, a table was erected and everyone took their seats.

"Don't worry! I haven't done sprouts." They all laughed. "But it's lovely to be back. And I wanted to share with you my interpretation of a... a Thismas dinner."

And it was wonderful. It couldn't have been anything else. It was Thismas. And Thismas means appreciating what we have before us and who is with us. It means appreciating this. Everyone loved the meal. Everyone ate far too much. Terry stood up to make a speech at the end of the meal. However, he looked around and saw that everyone was deep in conversation. Many were telling jokes. The elderly elves had fallen asleep on the couch and were snoring loudly.

"Now this feels like Christmas."

Tilly grinned. "Did we get it right?"

"I think you did. Listen, Tilly. I need to apologise. I think I've been too obsessive with my work."

"You reckon?"

"Well, I have. I don't want to miss this. I don't know how long this lockdown thing is going to last, but when it's over, I'm going to come back to Elfwood every weekend."

Tilly's jaw dropped. "Do you mean it?"

"I do."

"Oh Terry, that's wonderful news! Come here." And she gave him a big cuddle.

The next morning, Tilly shook Terry awake. "Psst. Terry. Come on."

"Where are we going?" She was already flying him into the sky.

"We're going back to the humans, of course."

"Oh. Are we?"

"Of course, we are, silly. It's Thismas day!"

"But it was Thismas day yesterday."

"Exactly! Isn't it such a wonderful holiday! It's always Thismas Day!"

But when they arrived, they saw that the children were sneaking about the house. They got closer to see what they were doing. Lou was sweeping in the hall. Erin and Charlie were in the kitchen, making breakfast.

"They're doing housework?" asked Tilly.

"That's not all they're doing!" shouted Terry, excitedly. "Don't you see why they're doing it?"

"To make the house nice and shiny? We don't really bother with sweeping in Elfwood. The trees get too dirty."

"Yes, I noticed." said Terry. "No, they're doing the housework for their parents. This is a very difficult time for them. Mr Kringle has to do his work in the living room and they both have to look after their children all the time. When they wake up, they'll have breakfast and coffee prepared and the house will be lovely and tidy. Their parents will get to enjoy their lovely day at home."

"They're going to have a lovely Thismas day."

Terry nodded. "A wonderful Thismas day indeed."

By this point, the children were sat in the bed with their parents. Mrs Kringle was eating some toast with jam. She loves raspberry jam. Mr Kringle was sipping his black coffee and telling a joke to his family. It is his favourite joke. He had read it in a Christmas cracker many Christmases ago and it is absolutely terrible. The elves smiled and left them to their joy.

As they were leaving, Terry said, "I meant to ask. What was in that package that you gave to Charlie for his birthday?"

"Oh, that? That's something very special."

"What is it?"

"It's a mirror. A magic mirror. I snuck the other into their grandparents' home. When the children look into it, they'll be able to speak to their grand-parents. It's what they want more than anything."

* * *

A period of time (which I am not at liberty to divulge) later, the lockdown was lifted and it was time for Terry to go home. Everyone was sad to see him go, not least because he was now shaping up into a wonderful cook. Tilly insisted on walking him to the edge of the Elfwood and she gave him a huge cuddle and a teeny tiny kiss when they got there.

"Thank you so much for everything Terry."

"You're welcome. It was wonderful to spend this time with you all."

"You will come visit again, won't you?"

"Every week."

"You must be very excited to get back."

"I am. Very excited. I can't wait to get back into the workshop. But," Terry smiled widely, "Elfwood will always be my home."

"Oh Terry." She grabbed him into another great big cuddle. "Now, get out of here before I cry."

Terry picked up his suitcase, said goodbye, and carried on up the hill towards the human world and then to the North Pole. On his one final journey back, Terry could not pass up the opportunity to see the Kringles one last time.

But the Kringles were not home. They were not in bed. They were not in their bedrooms. They were not doing housework. Terry checked his mirror, for Tilly had given him one to stay in touch.

"Show me Lou, Charlie and Erin Kringle."

And there they were. They were at a different house. They were running and laughing in the garden with a man and woman who both had white hair. The old man picked Lou up and gave her a big kiss on the cheek. Charlie was wearing a huge blue badge on his shirt that had a big number 10.

THANK YOU FOR READING

Dear reader,

I hope that you enjoyed reading Terry the Terrible Elf and Terry the Terrible Elf: Lockdown. It was certainly a lot of fun to write!

If you liked this book, please consider heading over to Amazon and leaving a review. It only takes a few minutes and it really, really helps.

As you know, self-published authors like myself rely heavily on recommendations from our our readers to get our books noticed by more people.

One more time, thank you so much for reading this book! You're amazing! Merry Thismas!

Joshua Potts